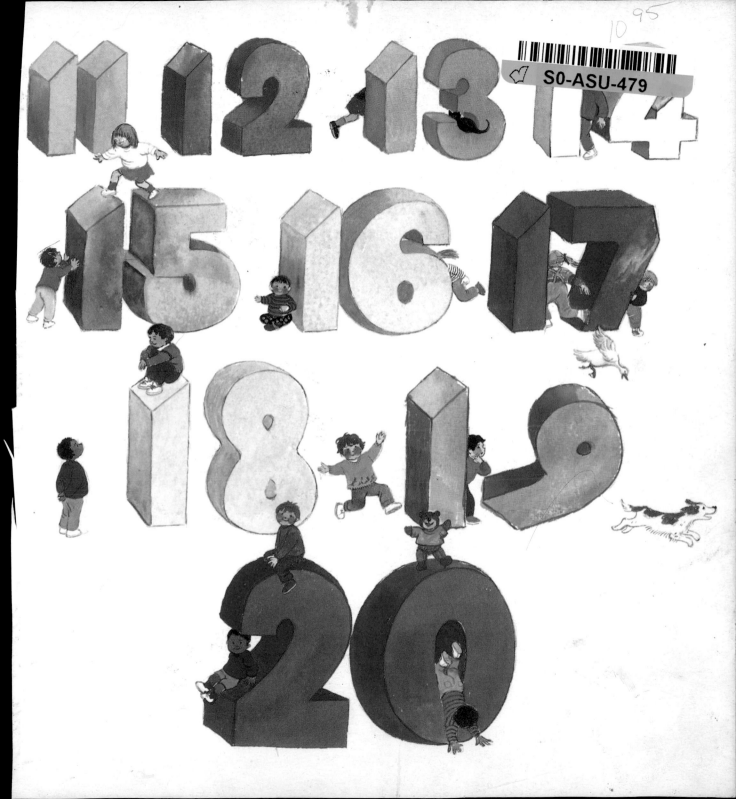

For Alexander

First published in the United States 1992 by
Dial Books for Young Readers
A Division of Penguin Books USA Inc.
375 Hudson Street
New York, New York 10014

Published in Great Britain by J. M. Dent & Sons Ltd.
Copyright © 1991 by Jenny Williams
All rights reserved
Printed in Italy
First Edition
1 3 5 7 9 10 8 6 4 2

Library of Congress Cataloging in Publication Data
Williams, Jenny, 1939–
Playtime 123 / Jenny Williams.
p. cm.
Summary: An introduction to counting through the depiction
of everyday activities.
ISBN 0-8037-1077-1 (trade)
[1. Counting.] I. Title. II. Title: Playtime one two three.
QA113.W55 1992
513.5'5—dc20 [E] 91-4683 CIP AC

The art for each picture consists of a
watercolor painting, which is scanner-separated
and reproduced in full color.

PLAYTIME

1 2 3

Jenny Williams

Dial Books for Young Readers · New York

boy hugs his teddy bear

2

delight in racing by

3 whiz down the slippery slide

4 swing upward toward the sky

5

fast riders on the go

6 young climbers bravely try

7 splashing in the pool

8  slick swimmers getting dry

9 go on a Sunday picnic

10 bear-buddies eat in the sun

 **11** arrive for a birthday party

12 **are playing, having fun**

13

jumping in the waves

14

caught by the camera's eye

15 hunt for seaside treasure

16 make castles and mudpies

17 listen to a story

18 play or read inside

at the merry-go-round

0 1 2 3 4 5